FALMOUTH AREA LIBRARY

W9-BOM-801

Best Friends
Get Better

Best Friends Get Better

Sandy Asher

Illustrations by
Sheila Hamanaka

A
LITTLE APPLE
PAPERBACK

SCHOLASTIC INC.

New York Toronto London Auckland Sydney

No part of this publication may be reproduced in whole or in part,
or stored in a retrieval system, or transmitted in any form or by any means,
electronic, mechanical, photocopying, recording, or otherwise,
without written permission of the publisher.
For information regarding permission, write to Scholastic Inc.,
730 Broadway, New York, NY 10003.

ISBN 0-590-41843-2

Copyright © 1989 by Sandy Asher.
All rights reserved. Published by Scholastic Inc.
APPLE PAPERBACKS is a registered trademark of Scholastic Inc.

12 11 10 9 8 7 6 5 4 3 2   0 1 2 3 4/9

Printed in the U.S.A.   11
First Scholastic printing, September 1989

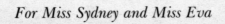
For Miss Sydney and Miss Eva

Contents

Best Friends
Get Better

Chapter One
People Change

Ellie Bell dashed up the stairs to David Sims' back door. Mr. Sims opened it even before she knocked.

"Good morning, Ellie," he said.

Ellie poked her glasses up on her nose. "Good morning, Mr. Sims," she said. "Can David come out and play?"

David was Ellie's best friend. He lived next door.

"David's at Ralph Major's house," said Mr. Sims. "He's spending the weekend there. He'll see you on Monday."

"Oh," said Ellie. "Okay."

She and David would begin third grade together on Monday. They went to Rountree School. So did Ralph. But Ralph was *not* Ellie's friend.

Ellie said good-bye to Mr. Sims and went home.

Ellie's mother was working in the kitchen. She had taken all the pots and pans out of the cabinets and was wiping down the shelves. The Bells always cleaned house on Saturdays.

"Where's David?" asked Mrs. Bell.

"At Ralph Major's house," said Ellie.

"Ralph Major?" asked Mrs. Bell. "Isn't he the boy who sat next to you last year? In the back row? The one who used to kick you?"

"Yes," said Ellie.

"I didn't know he was David's friend," said Mrs. Bell.

"Me, neither," said Ellie. "I didn't know he was anybody's friend. He's mean."

"Maybe he's changed," said Mrs. Bell. "People do change."

"Maybe," said Ellie. "But I still don't have anyone to play with."

Then she got an idea. "I could call Mary Stone. Will you drive me to her house to play?"

Mary was Ellie's other best friend. She lived eleven and a half blocks away.

"Have you cleaned your room?" Mrs. Bell asked.

"Yes," said Ellie.

"Okay," said Mrs. Bell. "Give Mary a call."

Ellie skipped over to the phone on the kitchen wall. She dialed Mary's number. Mary answered right away. But she couldn't play, either.

"I have to get ready for Ballet One," she said.

"What's Ballet One?" asked Ellie.

"It's a dance class," Mary explained.

"Every Saturday afternoon. I went last week. I loved it. Ballet One is for beginners. Then there's Ballet Two and Ballet Three and Ballet Four and Ballet Five."

"That's a lot of ballet," said Ellie.

"I'm going to be in Ballet Five some day," said Mary. "I'm going to wear beautiful costumes and dance on a stage."

"You are?" asked Ellie.

"Yes," said Mary. "We could do it together. You want to?"

"Me?" asked Ellie.

"Sure," said Mary. "But I have to go to the mall now. I just wore shorts last week because it was my first time. Now I need a leotard and tights. Pink. And ballet shoes. You could just wear shorts this time. Ask your mom. 'Bye."

Ellie hung up the phone slowly. A dance class with Mary? she thought. Beautiful costumes on a stage?

"Can I go to Ballet One?" she asked her mother.

Mrs. Bell pulled her head out of the cabinet under the sink.

"I thought you were going to see Mary," she said.

"I am," said Ellie. "At Ballet One. Can I go?"

Mrs. Bell was quiet for a moment. Ellie held her breath. "If it's okay with Daddy," said Mrs. Bell, at last.

Ellie ran down the basement steps to ask her dad.

Mr. Bell was stuffing old paint cans into a trash bag.

"Can I go to Ballet One?" Ellie asked him. "Mary is going. She loves it."

Mr. Bell shrugged. "If it's okay with Mom," he said.

"Thanks!" said Ellie, and flew back up the stairs. "He said yes," she told her mother.

Mrs. Bell called Mary's mom and got all the details. Then she called the ballet school. "Miss Drew says she has room for you in Ballet One," she told Ellie.

"Hooray!" Ellie cried. She couldn't wait to get there. Mary would be so surprised!

Chapter Two
Two Surprises

After lunch, Mrs. Bell drove Ellie to the South Oaks shopping center. She pulled into an empty space in the parking lot. Ellie read the sign over the door in front of them: MISS DREW'S SCHOOL OF DANCE. Tingly feelings wriggled from her head to her toes.

Mrs. Bell held the door open for Ellie. Miss Drew's School of Dance was a big, bright room. A row of mirrors ran all the way down one wall.

Ellie blinked. She could hardly see. But she could smell. "It smells like sweaty feet in here," she said.

FALMOUTH AREA LIBRARY

"Shhhhhh," said Mrs. Bell.

At last Ellie's eyes got used to the bright room. She saw a piano at the back. And there were children sitting on the floor. Four girls and two boys.

The girls wore pink leotards and tights. They were putting on their ballet shoes. The boys wore white T-shirts and black tights. Their shoes were black.

Ellie felt strange in her shorts and sneakers. She was wearing her Rountree T-shirt, but these children didn't go to Rountree. She didn't know any of them. Where was Mary?

Just then the front door burst open and Mary rushed in. "Hi, Mrs. Bell!" she cried. "Ellie, you're here!"

"Surprise!" said Ellie, with a big grin.

Then she noticed that Mary wasn't alone. There was another girl in the doorway. She was frowning at Ellie.

19

"This is Pat Parker," Mary said. "She just moved in on my block from across town. And guess what? She's going to be in third grade with us."

Ellie thought Pat Parker looked like the moon. She had a round moon face and pale moon hair. She wore her hair in two bunches of curls. They were tied in pink ribbons to match her leotard and tights.

"Are you new in Ballet One, too?" Ellie asked her.

Pat scrunched up her face and looked disgusted. "I've been in Ballet One all summer," she said. "I told Mary about it. That's why she's here." She tugged on Mary's arm. "Come on, Mary," she said. "Let's warm up for class."

"I want to show Ellie around first," Mary said.

Pat frowned harder. Then she turned on her heel and walked away.

"What's wrong with her?" Ellie asked Mary.

"I don't know," Mary said. "She's usually very nice."

A door opened behind the piano. A woman wearing ballet clothes came out.

"That's Miss Drew," said Mary. "Isn't she pretty?"

"Yes!" Ellie agreed.

Miss Drew was tall and thin. Her dark hair was pulled back tight. She smiled and said hello to all the children. The edges of her little black skirt rippled as she crossed the wide, wooden floor. "Hello, Mary," she said. "And you must be Ellie. And Mrs. Bell."

Miss Drew took Ellie's hand. She didn't smell like the room. She smelled good, like roses.

"Welcome to Ballet One," she said. Then she talked to Mrs. Bell for a while.

Miss Drew's skin was brown like David Sims'. Her eyes were big and black like David's. Ellie wondered if David was having fun at Ralph's house. He'd tell her all about it on Monday. And she'd tell him all about Ballet One.

"See you in an hour, Ellie," said Mrs. Bell.

Ellie waved good-bye. Mary and Miss Drew led her toward a long wooden pole on the wall across from the mirrors.

"This is the *barre*," said Miss Drew. "We hold onto the *barre* sometimes to help us do exercises. The first class is hard, Ellie. You'll need a little special help."

"I'll help her!" said Mary.

Miss Drew smiled. "Fine," she said. "We'll let Ellie stand right behind you." Then she clapped her hands. "Line up, class," she said.

Everyone hurried over to the *barre*. Pat

took the place in front of Mary. Class began. A man named Mr. Ross played the piano. He had big ears and a little bit of red hair.

Miss Drew led the class in exercises. They had strange names. Miss Drew said they were French.

"*Plié,*" she said.

Ellie followed Mary. They bent their knees like frogs.

"*Tendu,*" said Miss Drew.

They slid one foot in and out. It looked like they were mashing bugs on the floor. Ellie almost giggled. Ballet One was weird!

Sometimes they waved their arms. Sometimes they jumped up and down. It wasn't easy. But it wasn't too hard.

"From the corner, now," said Miss Drew.

The class left the *barre*. They lined up in the corner near the piano.

"What happens now?" Ellie asked.

"Walks and runs," said Mary. "You'll see."

"Shhhhh!" Pat Parker warned them.

Miss Drew stepped in front of the line. She walked across the room to peppy music. She held her head high. She swung her arms. She looked pretty.

One by one the class walked across the room. Ellie could tell they were trying to walk just like Miss Drew. Some did okay. Some were a mess.

Pat Parker was okay. Mary was the best. Ellie knew she would be. Mary was the fastest runner in their class at school. Even faster than the boys. Mary walked with her head high just like Miss Drew. She swung her arms. She looked very pretty.

It didn't even matter that her teeth stuck out. A lot. Mary smiled anyway. She always did.

"Very nice, Mary," said Miss Drew.

Ellie tried to walk just like Mary and Miss Drew.

"Very nice, Ellie," said Miss Drew.

"Thank you," said Ellie. She squeezed into line behind Mary at the other end of the room.

"What's next?" she asked.

"Shhhhhh!" hissed Pat.

Ellie bit her lip to keep from talking back. She didn't want to fight. Ballet One

was too interesting. She fixed the barrette slipping out of her hair and watched Miss Drew.

Miss Drew led the class again. She skipped, and the class skipped, too. Then she galloped. Just like a horse! Ellie giggled and thought, who ever heard of a horse dancing?

Wait a minute, she thought. Horses do dance . . . sometimes.

"Who knows another way to travel across the room?" Miss Drew asked the class.

"I do!" said Ellie. She lifted one knee and then the other. She pranced across the room. Mr. Ross played circus music.

"A circus horse!" said Miss Drew. She pranced across the room after Ellie.

The class joined in. They lifted their knees high. They bobbed their heads. They whinnied and snorted. Even Pat. Ellie smiled at her, but Pat turned away.

Ellie pulled Mary aside. "Ask Pat what's wrong," she said. "Ask her why she doesn't like me."

"I'll try," Mary promised.

Chapter Three
Too Many Horses

"Let's be all kinds of circus animals," said Miss Drew.

Everyone in the class spoke up. Lynn asked to be a lion. Paul wanted to be an elephant.

"I'm an elephant, too," said the smaller boy. His name was Stanley. He and Paul were brothers.

"A circus needs lots of elephants," said Miss Drew.

While the others chose their animals, Mary whispered to Pat. And Pat whis-

pered back. Then Mary came over to Ellie.

"I asked her why she doesn't like you,"
she said.

"And?" asked Ellie.

"She says she just doesn't," said Mary.

"But why?" asked Ellie.

Before Mary could answer, Miss Drew
said, "How about you, Mary?"

"I'd like to be a horse," said Mary. "I
love horses."

"Good!" said Ellie. "We can be horses
together."

"I love horses, too," said Pat. "A circus
needs lots of horses."

Oh, no, thought Ellie.

"Three horses," said Miss Drew. "That's
enough. What else?"

"A circus needs monkeys!" shouted a
girl with red hair.

"Yes, it does, Nancy," said Miss Drew.

Ellie took Mary aside again. "Ask her this," she whispered. "How come if she doesn't like me, she wants to be a horse with me?"

"Okay," said Mary. She moved over toward Pat.

The last two girls were Rosa and Sarah. Rosa wanted to be a dog that did tricks. Sarah wanted to be a bear.

"Do bears dance?" asked Paul.

"Everything that moves can dance," said Miss Drew.

"Everything?" asked Ellie.

"Look," said Miss Drew.

She opened the curtain at the front window. She pointed at a tree in the middle of the parking lot. A pair of blue jays chased each other through its branches. Beneath them petunias swayed on their stems. A yellow butterfly flickered from flower to flower.

"It *is* like a dance!" said Ellie.

"Everything that moves can dance," said Miss Drew. "Now get ready for our circus parade."

The class hurried into line, laughing and barking and roaring. Nancy made a monkey noise: "Chee-chee-chee!"

Miss Drew held up her hand. Everyone got quiet. "What do we hear when we watch a ballet?" she asked.

Ellie wanted to answer the question. She liked the way Miss Drew said, "Very nice, Ellie," when she did things right. But she'd never seen a ballet.

"Music," said Pat.

"Right!" said Miss Drew. "Only music."

Pat smirked at Ellie. Ellie looked at Mary. Mary rolled her eyes. Then she

stepped up close to Pat. She whispered in Pat's ear.

Miss Drew nodded to Mr. Ross. He played the parade music again. Miss Drew moved around the center of the circle. She didn't say a word. But everyone knew what she was doing. She blew a whistle. She cracked a whip.

"You're the ringmaster!" Ellie cried.

"Yes!" said Miss Drew. "I told a story with my face and my body, didn't I? No words, no sounds at all, except the music. Let's all try it."

Miss Drew blew her whistle and cracked her whip. Mr. Ross played the music. One by one, the animals entered the ring, quietly.

Ellie looked in the mirror. Horses and elephants, a dog, a monkey, a bear, and a lion danced around the ringmaster. They seemed to float on the music! Ellie wished they could go on forever. But the music ended.

"A parade is only the beginning," said Miss Drew. "Next the animals do their acts. Next week, we'll work on a dance for each one. Think about it until then, okay?"

"Is it time to go already?" asked Ellie.

Miss Drew laughed and gave her a hug. "I'm glad you came today, Ellie," she said.

"Me, too," said Ellie. "This is fun!"

Mary slipped in beside Ellie. "I'm glad you came, too," she said.

Pat was in a corner, changing her shoes. "Did you ask her?" said Ellie.

"Yes," said Mary. "She said she doesn't want to be a horse with *you*. She just wants to be a horse with *me*."

"That's mean!" Ellie cried.

"I know," said Mary.

"Are you going to stay friends with her?" asked Ellie.

Mary sighed. "I don't know," she said. "She lives right on my block. She'll be in my car pool every day."

Ellie bit her lip and waited. Who would Mary choose?

"She's always nice to *me*," Mary went on. "I was sure she'd like you, too. I thought we'd all be friends together. Oh, I don't know what to do!"

Chapter Four
New Class,
New Seat, New Rules

First thing Monday morning, Mary rushed up to Ellie in the schoolyard. "My mom says I *have* to be friends with Pat," she said. "She's our neighbor. Her parents are divorced and she and her mom are all alone. And my mom doesn't have to drive me anywhere to play with her."

"Oh," said Ellie. "What do we do now?"

Mary shook her head. "I don't know why Pat's so mean to you," she said. "When I ask, she says, 'Just because.' But I want to be your friend, too,"

"Maybe I should talk to David about

this," Ellie said. "Everything gets better when I talk to David."

"Okay," Mary agreed.

The bell rang and they dashed across the yard.

"Walk, please," said Mrs. Long, the principal. She was greeting everyone at the door. "Big third-graders this year!" she said to Mary and Ellie. She winked as they hurried inside.

Mr. Crane, the third-grade teacher, lined everyone up around the room. Then he began assigning seats. David and Ralph were the last to arrive. Ralph pushed into the line and pulled David in with him.

Mr. Crane put Ellie in the first row, first seat. Good! No more sitting at the back, where she couldn't see anything. No more Ralph kicking her.

David got the second row, first seat. Right next to Ellie! Great! She could ask him about Pat.

Then Mr. Crane gave Ralph the seat behind Ellie. He put Mary two rows away. And he put Mary in front of Pat. Not so great after all.

Next everybody had to stand up and tell something about themselves.

"I spent the weekend with Ralph," said David. "We played basketball."

"I have a basketball hoop on my garage," Ralph said jumping up. Then he sat down so hard, his desk shot into Ellie's chair.

"Quit it!" Ellie cried.

"Ralph Major," said Mr. Crane. "Third-graders take their seats carefully."

"I spent the whole summer in St. Louis," said Jimmy Duke. "It's a lot bigger than Springfield."

"I spent three days in New York City," said Kim Reed. "It's bigger than *any place*."

"I went to Ballet One," said Ellie.

"So did I," said Mary.

"So did I," said Pat.

"Ballet One?" said Ralph. "Yuck!" He stuck his finger in his mouth and made a noise like throwing up. Some people laughed. Mr. Crane shot him an angry look.

After everyone had spoken it was time for math. No talking allowed. Ellie would have to wait to talk to David. The math was easy, second-grade stuff. Ellie zipped right through it.

"Third-graders," said Mr. Crane, "think with their heads. Not with their fingers."

Ellie put down her pencil. She fixed her loose barrette.

"Are you finished already?" asked David.

"Yes," said Ellie.

"David Sims," said Mr. Crane, from across the room. "Ellen Bell. Third-graders do their math quietly."

David rolled his eyes at Ellie. Ellie shrugged and checked over her work. Only two erased places.

Wait a minute. Another mistake. She forgot to borrow. She hid her hands under her desk. She thought with her head. But she checked with her fingers. The answer was seven. One more erased place.

Now what? she wondered. She looked around the room.

"Third-graders' eyes stay on their own work," said Mr. Crane, from way in the back.

Ellie wasn't sure she liked Mr. Crane. He wasn't at all like Miss Drew. He had white fuzzy hair. He wore a yellow bow tie with brown dots. And he had a lot of rules. Ellie counted them on her fingers:

Third-graders raise their hands before they speak.

Only two third-graders at a time in the restroom.

Third-graders —

"I'll never be finished," David whispered. "I'll get old and die here, doing this math."

"David Sims," Mr. Crane called again.

David faced front, away from Mr. Crane. He stretched his tongue out and crossed his eyes. He grabbed his neck. His head hit the desk. Thump! He played dead.

Ellie giggled.

"Ellie likes David," Ralph Major sang into her ear.

That was true. Ellie did like David. But the way Ralph sang it, it sounded bad.

"David Sims," Mr. Crane said. "Ellen Bell. Ralph Major. Do I need to change your seats? Settle down."

He said it softly. But he meant it. Ralph plopped back into his chair. David got to work on his math. Two rows over, Pat erased her paper so hard, she ripped it.

Ellie sighed. When would she ever get to talk to David?

Chapter Five
David Is Different

Ellie watched David do his math. He wrote a number. Then he erased it. Then he wrote another number. Then he erased it. Two erased places in two seconds.

Mr. Crane was writing at his big desk up front. He wrote very fast. He didn't erase at all. He didn't stay at his desk long. He strolled up one aisle and down the next. Now and then he leaned over someone's desk and whispered.

He never leans over my desk, Ellie thought. He never whispers to me.

Mr. Crane leaned over David's desk and whispered.

Ellie raised her hand. "What did you say, Mr. Crane?" she asked.

"This is just between David and me, Ellen," Mr. Crane told her. "This is private."

David will tell me at recess, Ellie thought. And then I'll tell him about Pat. We tell each other everything.

But by recess time, it was raining. Mr. Crane made them all put their heads down. He read them funny poems.

David fell asleep on his desk, with his mouth wide open. Ralph pretended to snore. He did it right behind Ellie's back, so Mr. Crane wouldn't see. Mr. Crane went on reading. But he shot Ralph another angry look.

After recess and spelling, it was finally time for lunch. Ellie jumped up and ran toward her cubby.

"Ellen Bell," Mr. Crane said. "Third-graders do not run in their classroom. We walk. Slowly."

Ellie walked slowly. Then she grabbed her lunch fast. The bag popped open. Her apple fell out. It rolled under a desk. By the time she found it, everyone else had lined up. David was first in line. Ellie was last.

"David!" she called. "Wait for me in the lunchroom!"

"Third-graders," said Mr. Crane, "line up with their mouths closed and their eyes open." He led the class to the lunchroom.

The seat across from David was empty. Ellie grabbed it. "What did Mr. Crane whisper to you?" she asked.

"Stuff," David said. He opened his tuna salad sandwich. He laid both sides flat on the table.

"What stuff?" Ellie asked.

"Just stuff," David said. He put aside

a leaf of lettuce and a slice of tomato. Then he closed up the sandwich and took a bite.

"What kind of stuff?" Ellie asked.

"Private stuff," said David.

"Best friends tell each other everything," Ellie said. "I have a lot to tell you."

David munched his sandwich. His cheeks got round and full. Then they got flat again. "No," he said. "Not everything."

Ralph Major threw his tray down at the end of the table. He sat down so hard the whole bench bounced. "David likes Ellie," he sang.

"I do not," said David.

"You don't?" asked Ellie. "But we're best friends."

"Boys can't be friends with girls," said Ralph. He slid the cheese out of his sandwich and ate it in one bite. "Not in third grade," he added, with his mouth full.

47

TALMOUTH AREA LIBRARY

"Why not?" asked Ellie.

"Because," said Ralph, "it's not allowed."

"It is, too," Ellie told him. "We're *best* friends. Aren't we, David?"

David poked a finger through his lettuce. He didn't say a word.

"Ellie likes David," Ralph sang.

"So what?" Ellie asked.

"Sew buttons," Ralph said. He laughed at his own joke. Then he flipped a lump of bread at Ellie. It hit her arm.

Ellie shrugged it away. She looked at David. He didn't say a word.

"What's wrong with you, David?" asked Ellie.

"Nothing," said David. But he didn't look up.

"You're different," said Ellie.

"No, I'm not," David said. "Leave me alone."

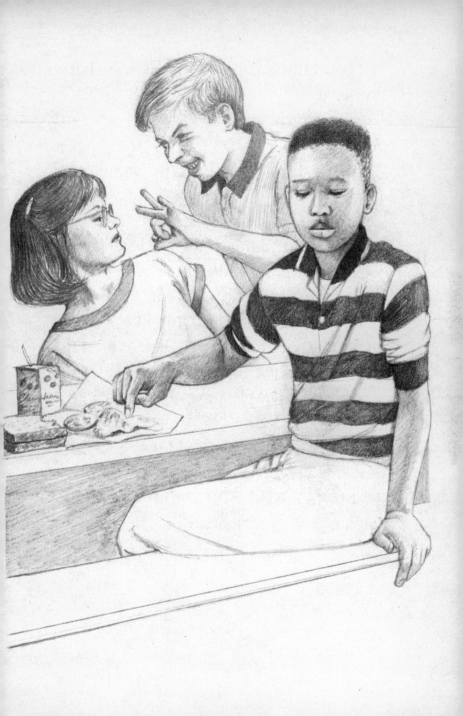

They finished their lunches with hardly another word.

After lunch, Ellie met Mary in the girls' room.

"What did David think we should do?" Mary asked.

"I didn't ask him," Ellie said. "I couldn't. He's changed. Sometimes people change."

"I guess so," said Mary. She tore her paper towel into tiny shreds. "I'm sorry, Ellie," she went on. "I still like you, but I have to be friends with Pat. And I like her, too — when she's not around you."

"Why do people have to change?" Ellie asked.

"I don't know," said Mary. "Maybe so they can get better."

"Maybe," said Ellie. "But what if they just keep getting worse?"

Chapter Six
Ralph Moves Up

"When people change," Ellie asked her mother the next morning, "do they get better? Or worse?"

Mrs. Bell stopped stirring the oatmeal and thought about it. "Sometimes better. Sometimes worse," she said at last. "Sometimes they get worse first, and then they get better. You just have to wait and see. And try not to worry."

"Oh," said Ellie. "Okay."

After breakfast she walked to school alone. David had left without her. Mary and Pat drove by in Mary's mom's car.

Mary waved. Ellie waved back. She tried not to worry about David or Mary or Pat. She told herself to wait and see.

At school she just did her work. She finished the math first again. No mistakes. But there were five erased places. She'd have to work on that.

"You're always the first one finished," said David. "You're just like my brother. Dad says he's a math whiz."

Ellie checked around for Mr. Crane. He was way across the room. "What's a math whiz?" she whispered.

"Someone who's great at math," David said. He made it sound bad, like Ralph did.

Ellie could see erased places all over David's paper. He tried to cover them up with his arm.

Ralph tapped her on the shoulder. Ellie turned around. He stuck out his tongue.

"Pthhhhhht," he said. Spit bubbles landed on his desk.

Ellie faced front again. She felt like crying. Ralph was just as bad as last year! And everybody else was getting worse! It was *hard* not to worry.

"Ellen?"

Ellie jumped. It was Mr. Crane. He was leaning over her desk. He was whispering to her!

"I see you've finished your math," he said. He smelled like peppermint. He ran his finger over her math paper. "Correct," he said. "Every one."

"There are too many erased places," Ellie told him.

"Don't worry about that," he said.

He took a red pen from his shirt pocket. *Great job, Ellen!* he wrote at the top of her paper. Mr. Crane wrote neatly. He never erased.

"The others need time to catch up with you," he went on. "While you're waiting, you may read this book."

"Thank you," said Ellie.

"You're welcome," said Mr. Crane.

He moved out of Ellie's row and into the next. Ellie wished he wouldn't go. She liked his peppermint smell. She liked the way he wrote her name. Ellen.

She looked down at the book he'd left on her desk. It was called *A Very Young Dancer*. It had lots of pictures. And it had a story about a girl who took ballet lessons. Just like Ellie!

The girl got to be in a real ballet on the stage. It was called "The Nutcracker." She wore beautiful costumes. But in her

dance class, she did the same exercises Ellie did in Ballet One. They even had the same French names.

David leaned across the aisle. "What's that?" he asked.

Ellie almost told him. She almost handed the book right over so he could see. Then she remembered. David was keeping a secret from her. He was acting mean, like Ralph. She slid the book off the desk and into her lap. "It's private," she said.

She turned to the next page. Somehow the book didn't seem as nice as before. Reading it made her feel lonely. She really hated not talking to David.

She gave his arm a poke. "David," she whispered.

"Ellen Bell," Mr. Crane said from three rows away. "Please let David do his math. You have a book to read."

"Can I show it to David?" Ellie asked.

"*May* I show it to David," said Mr. Crane.

"May I show it to David?" asked Ellie.

"After he finishes his math," said Mr. Crane.

David moaned. "I'll never get to see it," he said.

"Never say never, David," Mr. Crane told him. "Someday you will. If you get back to work. If Ellen lets you."

David tried. But his eyes wandered off his paper and across the aisle. Ellie could tell. Because he was her best friend.

Ellie brought the book up from her lap. She slid it across her desk. David's eyes wandered over. Ellie turned the pages. Dancers leaped and twirled.

"It's nice," said David.

Ellie nodded and turned another page.

"I see I've made a mistake," Mr. Crane said. "A mistake in the seating chart. Ralph,

would you please change seats with Ellen?"

"All right!" shouted Ralph.

"Quietly, please," Mr. Crane told him.

Ellie cleaned out her desk. She didn't
look at Mr. Crane. She didn't look at anybody. She was too ashamed. Ralph stood
next to her desk. He kicked her leg.

"Quit it," she said.

"Move it," he told her. "I sit next to
David now."

Chapter Seven
No Room for Ellie

"Line up, third-graders," said Mr. Crane.

It was time for recess. Ellie tucked the ballet book under her arm.

"Ellen Bell," said Mr. Crane. "Library books stay indoors."

Ellie sighed. She left the book on her desk. Then she hurried outside after David. He and Ralph raced across the yard.

"Wait for me!" Ellie yelled.

David slowed down. Ralph kept on running. Ellie caught up to David. "I showed you my book," she said.

"I know," said David.

"I got in trouble for it," Ellie said.

"I know," said David.

"So tell me your secret," said Ellie. "Tell me what Mr. Crane whispered."

"No," said David.

Ralph circled back to them. "Are you bugging my friend?" he asked Ellie.

"Is he your friend?" Ellie asked David.

"Sure," said David.

"Your best friend?" asked Ellie.

David looked at his feet.

Ralph answered for him. "Sure," he said.

"Can't you talk for yourself, David?" Ellie asked.

David didn't answer.

"We used to talk about *everything*!" Ellie cried. "Now you won't talk at all!"

Ellie ran away, as fast as she could. She ran as far as she could get from Ralph and David.

Then she stopped and looked around. Over by the swings, Pat was talking to Mary. Mary used to be *her* best friend. David used to be her best friend, too. Now they both had new friends and there was no room for Ellie!

Third-graders are a pain! she decided. She slipped around a corner to a little grassy place. It wasn't big enough to play in. Hardly anyone ever went there. No one was there now.

Good, she thought. She didn't want to see any more third-graders. She didn't even want to think about them. She sat on a tree stump and tried to think of something else. Her barrette was dangling in her hair. She pinned it back.

Miss Drew said to think about a dance for the Ballet Circus. Ellie tried to remember the circus she'd seen long ago. What had the horses done?

She stood up and pranced in a circle.

She tossed her head and made a bow. She twirled around a few times. She tried to leap like the dancers in her book.

Suddenly a ball bounced right between her feet. It rolled to a stop on the grass. David and Ralph dashed around the corner after it.

"What are you doing?" Ralph asked.

"Nothing," said Ellie.

"It looked like a dance," said David.

He smiled at Ellie. She couldn't help smiling back.

"It was a dance," she said. "I'm practicing for Ballet One. I wanted to tell you about it, David. I'm a horse."

"A dancing horse?" Ralph yelped.

"Horses dance," said Ellie. "In the circus. There's a lion, too, and elephants. Miss Drew is the ringmaster."

"That sounds like fun," David said.

"It is — " Ellie tried to tell him. But Ralph broke right in.

"That sounds dumb," he said. He began to sing: "Ellie-belly-smelly-jelly. Ellie's a dancing horse."

He skipped around Ellie. He flapped his hands in her face. He crossed his eyes and wiggled his tongue.

Ellie turned her back on him. "This is your last chance, David," she said. "Do you want to hear about Ballet One? Do you want to be my friend or not?"

David looked at Ralph.

"Dumb," said Ralph. "Girls are dumb. Dancing is dumb. And Ellie is double dumb."

David looked at his feet.

"All right for you, David Sims," said Ellie. "And this time I really, really mean it!" She walked away.

But Ralph followed her. And David followed Ralph.

"Ellie-belly-smelly-jelly," sang Ralph.

"Ellie-belly-smelly-jelly," sang David. He

didn't sing it very loud. But he sang it.

Ellie walked faster. The boys walked faster. They sang louder. Ellie ran. The boys ran after her, singing even louder. Ellie covered her ears with her hands.

"Shut up!" she shouted.

Mrs. Long crossed the yard in giant steps. "Ralph! Ellie! David!" she called after them. "That is quite enough."

Chapter Eight
Pat Needs Special Help

For the rest of the week, Ellie tried to wait and see. She tried not to worry. But there was nothing new to see on Wednesday. Or Thursday. Or Friday.

On Saturday, she was glad to be alone in her room, even if she did have to clean it.

"Aren't you going over to David's house?" Mrs. Bell asked Ellie, as she put fresh sheets on Ellie's bed. "You haven't been there all week."

"No," said Ellie.

Mr. Bell peeked in at the door. "You haven't tied up the phone all week, either," he said. "Aren't you going to call Mary?"

"No," said Ellie.

"Are you going to tell us what's wrong?" asked Mrs. Bell.

"No," said Ellie. She couldn't. She didn't *know* what was wrong. Maybe Pat knew. Maybe David knew. But no one was telling *her*.

At last it was time for Ballet One. "I want to wear my hair like Miss Drew," Ellie said. "So my barrettes don't keep falling out."

"All right," said Mrs. Bell. "Get dressed first."

While she changed into her new pink leotard and tights, Ellie thought about her dance for the Ballet Circus. She had practiced it in her room after school every day. After she slipped on her new ballet shoes, she decided to practice it once more.

Mrs. Bell fixed Ellie's hair. Mr. Bell drove her to Miss Drew's School of Dance. Ellie hurried inside.

The room was filled with the same brightness and the same funny smell of feet. Ellie was glad. She remembered the names of all the children who were there. "Hi, Rosa," she said. "Hi, Paul. Hi, Stanley."

No Mary or Pat yet. Good.

Miss Drew came out of her office. "Hello, Ellie," she said. "Warm up, everyone. We'll start soon. Ellie, come to the *barre* and let me check your new ballet shoes."

Ellie ran to the *barre* with the others. When Mary and Pat arrived, Miss Drew was poking the tips of Ellie's ballet shoes.

"A perfect fit!" she said.

Mary smiled at Ellie. Ellie smiled back, just a little.

Class began. Ellie remembered all the exercises. She even remembered their French names. Mr. Crane's book helped. *Plié*. That was when you bent your knees like a frog. *Tendu*. That was sliding your foot, like mashing bugs. And the little jumps were called *changements*.

After the *barre* exercises, they did more walks and runs from corner to corner. Then it was time for the ballet circus.

"Our parade is all set," said Miss Drew. "Now the animal acts begin. Has anyone thought about it?"

Ellie's hand flew into the air. So did Mary's. They were the only ones. Then Pat raised her hand, too.

"I forgot," said Paul.

"Me, too," said Stanley.

"That's okay," said Miss Drew. "You'll

all have time to work on your dances soon. But first let's see what these three have to show us. Who wants to go first?"

Ellie wasn't sure. She couldn't wait to show Miss Drew her dance. But she couldn't get her hand to go up again, either.

Miss Drew chose Mary. Her dance was good, but kind of short. Everyone clapped for her.

"Very nice, Mary," said Miss Drew. Then she nodded at Ellie.

Ellie pranced in a circle. Then an empty feeling filled up her head. A lumpy feel-

ing flopped over in her stomach. She forgot what came next!

Somehow her feet remembered. They did everything she'd practiced. In no time her dance was over. It was even shorter than Mary's. But everyone clapped.

"Very nice, Ellie," said Miss Drew. "Pat?"

Pat took a step forward. Then she took a step back. "I don't remember my dance," she said.

"Maybe if you begin," said Miss Drew, "it will come back to you."

"No," said Pat. "It won't."

"I don't think she ever had a dance," said Nancy. "I think she just said that to be like Mary."

"I did too have a dance," said Pat, blushing.

"That's enough," said Miss Drew. "Mary and Ellie, you two and Pat are all circus horses. I'd like you to help her with her dance. I'll work with the rest of the class."

Mary took Pat's hand and led her toward a corner of the room. Ellie shuffled after them. Last week she had needed special help. This week she was a special helper. That was good. But did she have to help *Pat*?

Chapter Nine
Golden Sun, Silver Moon, and Daisy

"I'm calling my horse Daisy," Ellie said when she caught up with Mary and Pat.

"Mine is Golden Sun," said Mary.

"Mine's Silver Sun," mumbled Pat. She kept her eyes on the floor.

"Yours can't be Silver Sun," Ellie told her. "It's too much like Mary's. And anyway the sun isn't silver."

Pat's bottom lip popped out. Ellie heard her sniffle.

"It doesn't matter what we're called," Mary said. "Your dance is what matters."

"I don't want Ellie to help me," Pat said.

"Miss Drew says I have to," said Ellie.

"Besides," said Mary, "we're all circus horses. We all should be friends."

"She's not my friend," Pat shouted. "And if you want to dance with her, you're not my friend, either."

Suddenly Ellie felt a hand on her shoulder. "We all work together here," said Miss Drew. "Or there will be no ballet circus. You three go into my office and settle this. Through that door behind the piano. Quickly and quietly."

Mary hurried into the office. Ellie and Pat trudged in after her. When Mary turned around, her eyes were wide and shiny. She started to cry.

"I don't like being in the middle," she said. "And I don't want to choose. You're both my friends. Why can't you be friends with each other?"

"We just can't," said Pat.

"Why not?" asked Mary.

"I was friends with Mary before you even met her," said Ellie.

"I know that," Pat snapped. She began to cry, too. "Mary started talking about you the minute I moved in: Ellie's smart and Ellie's nice and Ellie's this and Ellie's that."

Mary sniffed. "I like Ellie," she said.

"Then that leaves me out," said Pat.

"No, it doesn't," said Mary.

"Yes, it does," said Pat. "You two are good dancers and I'm not. You got your dances perfect the first time. I can't even make one up."

"Then you really didn't have a dance?" asked Ellie.

"I had one," said Pat. "But it was dumb."

"I'll bet it wasn't," said Mary. "Remember what Miss Drew said? Everything that moves can dance."

"Even petunias," Ellie added.

FALMOUTH AREA LIBRARY

"I guess I can dance better than a petunia," Pat admitted. Ellie giggled. Pat smiled at her. But it faded quickly. "I'm too scared to do my dance alone," she said.

"I was scared," said Ellie.

"Me, too," said Mary.

"You were?" asked Pat.

"Everybody gets scared," said Ellie.

"I thought I was the only one," said Pat.

"Oh, no!" said Mary and Ellie together. They gave each other a knowing look.

"Everybody worries about not being good enough," said Mary. "I thought my dance was too short."

"Mine, too!" said Ellie. "Maybe we should put all our short dances together. Then we'd have one long dance. And we wouldn't have to do it alone."

"Could we?" asked Pat.

"If you want," said Ellie.

"I do if you do," said Pat.

"You know *I* do!" cried Mary. She grinned at them both.

Ellie and Pat grinned back. Then they looked at each other.

"Silver Moon," said Ellie. "That's a nice name for your horse, Pat."

"It is," said Pat. "Thanks, Ellie."

Miss Drew came to the door. "How are we doing in here?" she asked.

"Fine!" answered Ellie and Mary and Pat.

Miss Drew laughed. "You don't have to *talk* together," she said. "Just work together."

Giggling, they followed her out of the office.

Miss Drew called everyone together. "In one month," she said, "we'll have Visiting Day. Your families are invited to watch class. We'll show them everything you've learned so far. And we'll perform our Ballet Circus."

"For friends, too?" asked Ellie.

"Friends, too," said Miss Drew.

"Let's invite the whole class!" said Mary.

"You want to, Ellie?" asked Pat.

David! thought Ellie. But would he come?

She looked at Mary and Pat. They were waiting for her to say yes. They were all friends now. It felt nice. Ballet One was more than dancing. It was good feelings and friends.

"Yes!" she said. She would ask David herself. She wanted him to be a friend, too.

Chapter Ten
A Spider
and Special Math

David was at Ralph's house for the weekend again. Ellie had to wait till Monday to invite him to Visiting Day at Ballet One. Monday morning she ran all the way to school.

David was already in his place when she got there. So was Ralph, right next to him. The minute Ellie took her seat, Mr. Crane began to call the roll. No talking allowed.

Ralph dropped something over his shoulder. It fell onto Ellie's desk. It was a spider. A big, black, wiggly spider. Ellie knew it was fake. But it was still creepy.

"Quit it, Ralph," she whispered.

"Ellen Bell. Ralph Major," Mr. Crane said. "Do I need to change your seats again?"

Ellie wished he would. She wished he would change her seat back to the one next to David's. She wished he would change Ralph's seat to one on Mars.

Mr. Crane went on calling the roll. Ellie stuffed the spider down the back of Ralph's shirt.

"Quit it, Ellie!" Ralph snapped. He jumped out of his seat. He stuck his hand down his shirt and danced around. He really looked funny. Ellie covered her mouth to keep from laughing out loud.

"Ellie put a spider down my shirt," Ralph yelled.

"It was your spider," said Ellie.

Mr. Crane sighed. "Sit down, Ralph," he said.

Ralph sat down. Mr. Crane finished the roll. Then he pointed to the math assignment written on the board. Everyone got to work.

"David Sims," Mr. Crane said. "Kim Reed. James Duke. Please come up here."

Ellie watched David join the others at Mr. Crane's desk. Mr. Crane whispered to them for a while. Then they got their math books and left the room.

Ellie raised her hand. "Where are they going?" she asked.

"I know," Ralph called out. "Dummy math."

Mr. Crane gave Ralph an angry look. "It's called *special* math," he said. "Everyone needs special help sometimes."

Ellie raised her hand again. "My eyes need special help," she said. "Glasses."

"My teeth will need special help when I'm older," said Mary. "Braces."

"When I was your age," said Mr. Crane,

"I couldn't read or write. I needed special help, too."

"You sure write okay now!" said Ellie.

Mr. Crane laughed. "Thank you, Ellen," he said.

Pat raised her hand. "I needed special help in Ballet One," she said. "Ellie and Mary helped me. And Ellie named my horse."

"You don't have a horse," yelled Ralph.

"Ralph Major," said Mr. Crane, "please move your desk and chair right up here next to mine. Thank you."

Ralph moved his desk and chair. They squeaked along the floor. He grinned at the class and crossed his eyes.

"Your next move, Ralph," said Mr. Crane, "will be to Mrs. Long's office."

Ralph sat down in his new place, facing front. His head drooped. The back of his neck turned bright red. Ellie felt a little sorry for him.

FALMOUTH AREA LIBRARY

"Patricia," Mr. Crane said, "why did Ellen name a horse in a ballet class?"

Pat told him about the circus.

"In one month, we'll have Visiting Day," Ellie added. "Everybody who wants to can come."

Especially David, she thought. She raised her hand again. "When will those kids come back from special math?"

"They'll join us at recess," said Mr. Crane.

Ellie could hardly wait.

Chapter Eleven
People Change Again

David was already outside when Ellie got there. He was leaning against the fence, alone. Ellie ran up to him.

"Hi, David," she said. "How was special math?"

David's dark eyes got big and round. "How did you know?" he asked.

"Ralph told us," Ellie said.

"He wasn't supposed to," said David. "It's private."

Ralph Major ran up. "Dummy-tummy-rummy-gum," he sang. "David's in dummy math!"

"Quit it, Ralph," said David. "Some friend you are."

Ralph went right on singing. He skipped in a circle around David. He waved his spider in David's face.

Ellie pushed him away. Ralph pushed her back.

David punched Ralph on the arm. Ralph punched David in the face. David fell down. Ralph sat on top of him.

Ellie jumped on Ralph. She pulled him off David. She sat down on him. Hard.

"David! Ralph! Ellie!" shouted Mrs. Long. "Please get up."

Ellie stood up fast. So did David. Ralph took longer.

"What's this all about?" Mrs. Long asked.

"Ralph said David's in dummy math," said Ellie. "I just wanted him to know it was *special* math."

"And do you know that now, Ralph?" Mrs. Long asked.

"I guess," Ralph said.

"Then it's settled," said Mrs. Long. "No more fighting. Go find something better to do. All of you."

Ellie walked slowly toward the swings. Ralph went the other way. Ellie turned to see which way David would go. He caught up with her. For a while they were quiet.

Ellie climbed onto the first swing. David got on the second. They twisted the chains until they were tight. The swings spun them around, first one way, then the other.

"I'm sorry I made fun of you," said David at last. "And I guess I can tell you what Mr. Crane whispered to me last week. It was about special math. I didn't want you to know."

"Why not?" Ellie asked.

"You're the best in math," David said. "I felt bad."

"I was the best in math last year, too," Ellie said. "We were friends then."

"I didn't sit next to you last year," said David. "I didn't know you were always the first one finished. And I didn't have to be in special math."

"Everyone needs special help sometimes," Ellie said. "Mr. Crane said so. Even him. When he was in third grade, he couldn't even read or write."

"I didn't know that," said David.

"Me, neither," said Ellie. "But now I do."

Ellie stopped spinning and pushed her swing off straight. Higher and higher she went. David pumped hard to catch up with her.

"I still count on my fingers," she called to him.

"You do?" he asked.

"I make mistakes," Ellie said, "I have to erase them. Then I have to fix them."

"Me, too," said David. "Only I don't know how to fix them. That's what we're learning in special math."

"Good," said Ellie.

"But I wonder why my brother's a math whiz and I'm not," said David. "And my sister's a science whiz. Maybe they used up all the whiz before I was born."

"Maybe you're a different kind of whiz," said Ellie.

David looked sad. "Yeah," he said. "A special math whiz."

Ellie slowed her swing down. Her shoes scuffed the dirt. "David," she said, "I don't care if you're in special math. Or not-so-special math. I just want us to be friends."

David slowed down, too. He looked at Ellie and smiled. "We are," he said. "We're best friends."

"Good!" said Ellie. "And Mary and Pat are my best friends. They can be your friends, too. Okay?"

"Okay," said David. "And Jimmy Duke

and Kim Reed are my best friends. They can be yours, too."

"Okay," said Ellie.

Across the yard, Mr. Crane blew his whistle. Ellie and David jumped off the swings and started toward him. There was Ralph Major, over by the fence. He was mean. But seeing him alone made Ellie sad. David saw him, too.

"Ralph always ends up alone," Ellie said.

"He says boys and girls can't be friends," said David.

"Ralph doesn't know much about friends," said Ellie.

"I guess not," agreed David. "Maybe he needs special help."

Ellie nodded, laughing. Everything got better when she and David talked about it. Even Ralph.

"Come on, Ralph," she yelled. "Time to go in." Ralph made a face. Then he headed over.

But there was one more thing Ellie

needed to tell David. "Visiting Day for Ballet One is in one month," she said. "Will you come?"

"Sure," said David. "What's it like there? What do you do?"

"Third-graders return from recess quietly," said Mr. Crane. He held a finger to his lips as the class lined up.

"I'll tell you all about it at lunch," Ellie whispered to David. "Miss Drew and the French names and everything."

"David Sims. Ellen Bell," said Mr. Crane.

Ellie and David grinned at each other and hurried inside together.